By Elijah Frederick

Contributions by: Leah Frederick

Edited by: Rachel Beckles

Illustrated by: Jeremy Salmon

Published in Great Britain by

Elijah Frederick

First printed 2021

For Mum and Grandad

Shifted Code: Hacked

Contents

Chapter 1

It was Tadeo's first day at his new school: Westwood High. The hallways seemed busier; the students seemed less friendly; most teachers didn't seem to care that he didn't know his way around. Secondary school was a lot bigger and more intense than primary school, but Tadeo was confident he could handle it.

His first lesson was Science class, his chance to shine. Tadeo sat on the edge of his chair. However, the other kids didn't really seem to come alive in science class. Despite this, science was one of his favourite subjects. Tadeo knew he wanted to have a career in science because he has always been passionate about it.

Tadeo also noticed that Nathan and his larger group of friends were in his science class, too. Most of them were bullies. There were actually bigger bullies than Nathan in Westwood that Tadeo noticed in his first days.

Nathan and Tadeo were the only two people from his primary who went to Westwood high. Although Tadeo and Nathan weren't friends, they had a mutual understanding at Westwood. This resulted from the respect they gained for one another whilst working on the computing project back in primary school.

"Name a feature unique to animal cells?" Mr Johnson asked.

"The nucleus," Tadeo raised his hand.

"Name a feature unique to plant cells?" Mr Johnson asked again.

"The cell wall." Tadeo, being the only person answering.

The next lesson was P.E. The changing rooms had an odour of stale urine that curled from under the restroom doors, depressingly mixed with deodorant and body odour in equal measure. Tadeo kept his head down and pushed his way through the sea of despondent faces. His P.E. class was told that because of poor weather, they were to do a theory lesson.

Eventually, he was dismissed and went straight into the art room for his next lesson. The lunch bell rang, and it freed Tadeo from art class. When Tadeo drew, it was like a six-year-old with a broken arm was given a crayon and told to have fun. His ideas were very creative, but he was never great at or enjoyed drawing.

Tadeo could see a gang of troublesome teenagers unwillingly wearing the school uniform performing the rebellious act of tying their burgundy jackets around their waists, which was against the school's policies. Taking advantage of not being under surveillance by a teacher, they messed around on their phones.

As he walked into the cafeteria alone, looking desperately for an empty table, someone tapped him on the shoulder.

"You look lonely," he smiled at Tadeo, "Would you like to eat with me?"

"That would be nice. Thanks," Tadeo replied.

"I'm Andre,"

"I'm Tadeo. Nice to meet you! What football team do you support?"

"Chelsea, you?"

"Arsenal," Tadeo sighed

"That's a shame. I was beginning to think you were a chill person," Andre joked. "But what are you into?"

"Gaming and stuff like that. Oh, and also reading! How about you?"

"Yeah, the exact same!" They both faintly smiled in agreement, which instantly solidified a new friendship.

Tadeo and Andre talked and talked and talked to get to know each other even more. They both shared even more interests and really wanted to thrive academically.

After lunch, Tadeo and Andre found themselves in the same classes for the rest of the day, which included Religious Studies and

English. Luckily, they both sat next to each other in Religious Studies. In English, they were on different tables, however still within talking distance.

The teacher dismissed Tadeo's class and as soon as he and Andre walked out of the class, they both sighed a breath of relief simultaneously. They both walked from their English class out of the school gate and parted ways at the top of the road. Tadeo walked to the bus stop like a king with a smile to everyone he passed.

After what felt like ages, Tadeo finally thought he could faintly see the bus in the distance. Inside, the passengers were a curious mixture of cosy and bored, all of them itching for their destinations. Tadeo got on and sat down on the first seat he saw. The bus was sleek, running over the black tarmac so fast that the passing greenery became a hazy blur. The windows became beaded, and the rain beat on the roof like a crazy drummer. Tadeo was just looking out of the window, observing his surroundings, trying to get used to his route from school. The Channel 7 statin stuck out like a splinter, with it being in eyeshot from the one bus stop on his way home – Tadeo made a mental note and knew he could now never get lost.

After what felt like ages, Tadeo finally thought he could faintly see the bus in the distance. Inside, the passengers were a curious mixture of cosy and bored, all of them itching for their destinations. Tadeo got on and sat down on the first seat he saw. The bus was sleek, running over the black tarmac so fast that the passing greenery became a hazy blur. The windows became beaded, and the rain began to beat on the roof like a crazy drummer. Tadeo was just looking out of the window, observing his surroundings, trying to get used to his route from school. The Channel 7 station stuck out like a splinter, with it being in eyeshot from the one bus stop on his way home – Tadeo knew he could now never get lost.

The bus stop wasn't far from his house, a five-minute walk at the most. Tadeo arrived at his house and ruffled his keys in the lock and after what seemed like hours, he got the door open. He instantly took off his shoes, and he bolted up the stairs like an Olympic champion at the start gun.

Getting changed out of his school clothes, Tadeo got changed into his casual tracksuit, which he always liked to wear in the house. Scavenging under his desk, Tadeo found the box that contained his old laptop, one which he was looking for. Tadeo got his Bluetooth speaker and started playing some afro beats. He just began typing and coding away - adding to an already complex project he always worked on. The project aims to scan any maths question in the world and find an answer whilst also providing a step-by-step process. He was so focused on building the program that he didn't hear the doorbell ring or the fact that his sister came into his room and stood behind him trying to get his attention!

"Tadeo!!!" she said

"Yes, Nia! Stop shouting at me. What do you want?" Tadeo lowered the volume on his speaker.

"Mum wants to speak to you."

"Tell her I'm coming, Nia! Can't you see I am working," Tadeo said, bickering with his sister.

"Ok whatever".

After finishing the last line of code for the section, he left his room and dashed down the stairs and entered the front room. His mum almost broke his back with the hug she gave him!

"So…How was your first day at school?" she asked

"Great actually. I made a new friend,"

"That's lovely to hear,"

Tadeo's mum left the room whilst Nia was glued to the TV, oblivious to everyone around her. Nia would always control the TV, but she wasn't allowed to until she had read for at least twenty minutes after school. Nia was in year two and attended the same primary school as Tadeo had moved on from.

Their mum called them both for dinner. The food surprised and somewhat confused Tadeo on his plate. Nia also had the same expression as him. Vegetarian pizza and chips were on their plate, whilst their mum had a pepperoni. Their mum was vegetarian and Nia loved peperoni pizza.

"Mum? Why have you got pepperoni, you're vegetarian?" Nia asked.

"It was a test to see how you both would react. And you passed it" their mum laughed.

Their mum switched hers and Nia's plate, but Tadeo still had vegetarian pizza. The doorbell rang and Tadeo went to answer. It was their dad! With cookie dough as a bonus.

Tadeo and his dad walked into the dining room and everyone apart from Tadeo laughed.

"You were never having vegetarian pizza, silly!" Nia giggled.

Tadeo told his mum and dad more about his day and his new school. Nia then told everyone that she got extra 'Golden Time' for being one of the best behaved in her class today. After they all ate, Tadeo went to finish building his robot and by then it was late. He had a shower and then went to sleep.

Whilst his first day at school seemed to go on forever, the rest of the week flew by. Friday came along in an instant, and Tadeo was feeling even better about school. He had a group of friends now that were all like him.

The wind howls as the students arrive through the gates, hustling and bustling down the corridors. Friends are greeting each other with a hug or a playful punch while the outcasts stand, looking scared. The older kids stand tall, proud and confident, born of experience. The bell rings and everybody hurries to line up, except for an occasional slowcoach or chatterbox.

The last lesson of the day was science. This classroom was Tadeo's salvation. When he walked in there, his mind could function, his stride grew longer and he could be himself. This is the place where he could learn, to explore and be with friends who really understand him. Somehow in this classroom, his differences were not only accepted, but celebrated. But not in every classroom. Most of the class weren't really bothered apart from Tadeo and three of his new friends: Marcel, Bradley and Jake, were all in his class. The lesson seemed to fly by. Mr Johnson dismissed the class and Tadeo walked out of the school with his new friends.

He invited a few friends round his house that Saturday whilst his parents were taking his sister to a dance showcase. Andre, Kiara, Marcel, Bradley and Jayda, all ended up coming and they played on the Gamechip 64.

"Which game should we play?" Jayda asked.

"I think we should play Endorscape. "It's my favourite," Tadeo suggested.

They had all taken turns and played single player on Endorscape, but none of them had completed the game, not even Tadeo! Eventually, Tadeo suggested they do multi-player on Endorscape and everyone agreed. Half an hour later, they got bored with playing because they just kept on losing, so everyone went outside to play football in the garden. With Tadeo turning off the TV and the Gamechip 64.

***

Chapter 2

When the console is off, the characters have their own minds and can roam around within the game. They cannot be controlled and are not bound by the laws of the code meaning they had free will.

Pupetra slumped back in her throne made of skeletons and overlooked the island whilst in deep concentration. She looked up and saw the viruses battling with the anti-viruses. It sounded like a world war dogfight was happening. She then clenched her fists and screamed out in anger.

After Tadeo got himself sucked into Endorscape, he installed a security app on the

Gamechip 64. The app produces anti-viruses and their job is to make sure viruses do not infect any of the games. The security app also created a dome separating every game Tadeo has built.

"There has to be a way." Pupetra muttered to her minions whilst banging her fist on the arm of her throne and banging a sceptre on the ground.

"What is it, empress?" one cyclops replied.

"Search the island. Whoever here is programmed to help Tadeo, find them and bring them to me!!!" Pupetra ordered.

At that command, a minotaur and a cyclops seemed to move like an agile unit ready to pounce on its next victim. They ran into the jungle like a menacing blur. The scraping of the cyclops' claws could be mistaken for noises coming from a construction site.

Cutting their way through the dense, suffocating undergrowth, fighting through the very air, which hung heavy, moist and still. Trees tall as cathedrals surrounded them. A strange green light, almost holy, shimmered through the vast blanket of leaves.

The minotaur and the cyclops noticed smoke coming from a campfire in the distance and headed in that direction, slowly but surely. Instead of hunting fast, it preferred to toy with its food . The meal would be allowed the chance to run, to feel the pounding of their own heart just a few more times before capturing the prey.

Infernore heard the snap of a twig and tried to scramble up his ladder into his tree fort and peered out of his window, only to meet the gaze of the two beasts, and if looks could kill, he would have been dead. The minotaur and the cyclops tied a nearby rope to the tree and pulled it like a tug of war.

"LEAVE ME ALONE!!!" Infernore shouted.

The tree collapsed like a feather within seconds of the minions pulling on the rope. An unconscious Infernore was seized by the minions that followed the cyclops and minotaur. They dragged Infernore back to

Pupetra on the mountain. Infernore was slammed on the floor. The minions in front of Pupetra looking down at him with a venomous smile. Until eventually, his eyes slowly flickered open.

"You are programmed to help Tadeo," Pupetra said with hatred.

"And? What is your point? Everyone knows what they are programmed to do." Infernore replied willingly, without restraining.

"Those viruses can delete people. Correct?" Pupetra pointed above to one of them roaming around. They could only be described as resembling a smudge on a painting.

"Yes, they can. The viruses have the power to delete people." Infernore began, his voice trembling.

"So how do I get them in this game?" Pupetra ordered and immediately Infernore looked away. "Tell me or I'll reduce you to dust!!!"

"A bunker... a secret bunker that leads to the code caves. My friend guards them. I will take you to him, alright?!" Infernore revealed.

"Good." Pupetra smirked.

Infernore stumbled to his feet and then led Pupetra to the code caves, but it was very well disguised. The gateway that led to the code caves was on the north side of the map.

It is uninhabited because of the virus attack that happened long ago.

They could spot a steeled door faintly over the hill they had just climbed. The door was covered with tangled overgrown trees, branches, thorns and what appeared to be boulders. Nevertheless, Infernore and Pupetra fought their way through it and were now face to face with the door.

Pupetra conjured dark energy and a ball of purple like fire flew from her hand and didn't even scratch the door. She repeated the same action again and again. Each time she failed, it created an even more untamed attempt.

"I'm putting in the code to open it," Infernore explained sarcastically while Pupetra scowled at him. The door hesitantly creaked open. "My friend Kylo. He will help you once you get down there."

The other cave walls on the island are usually covered in moss and ivy around here, but not in the code caves. No light means no plants. Instead, just old brick. Listening but not looking at Infernore, Pupetra stormed ahead into the code caves. It was a cave mouth of impenetrable blackness. As Pupetra stepped in, she watched her shadow dissolve into the surrounding darkness. As soon as she was out of sight, Infernore put the code back in and the door closed, sealing her inside.

Immediately, Infernore got out his walkie-talkie.

"Kylo, Kylo come in." Infernore panicked.

"Infernore! It's great to hear your voice. How have you been?" Kylo asked.

"Fine, fine. Listen up, Pupetra is coming in the code caves. I need you to find a way to trap her down there. Once you have done that, sneak your way back to me." Infernore told him

"Why? It's a risky plan." Kylo questioned.

"If we do this, it could be the end of Pupetra and we will all be free." Infernore explained.

"Ok I'm on it." Kylo replied.

Pupetra bumped into who she assumed was Kylo.

"I can't see. Light the way." Pupetra ordered Kylo.

And without a response, he pulled out two sticks from his pocket and rubbed them together and created a torch. In the cave, the only sound that met her straining ears was her own echoing footsteps. Kylo led Pupetra up a trail that had been created by many footprints.

Kylo lives within these caves. In the darkness, his blood regulated to a comfortable temperature.

"The further down you go within the cave, the more code you can access." Kylo explained, trying to lead a rat into a trap.

"I want to change the code to deactivate the dome and disable the anti-viruses. For all of the games Tadeo has created." Pupetra told Kylo.

"Well, if you want to do that, we must go to the depth of the cave itself because you want to change the code for all the games." Kylo replied.

The further they went down in the cave, the heavier the mud became on their feet, along with the fact that the air became hot and sticky. After what seemed like hours of walking, Kylo appeared to collapse in slow motion after presenting Pupetra with the S.A.C.C.

"This is the S-A-C-C, or Sacc, as I call it. It stands for the security app code controller. It is the control panel for the security app. It acts as both a creature and a machine. This would be able to disable the domes for all games as well as the anti-viruses... but only temporarily," Kylo told Pupetra.

"Whatever," she snapped dismissively. "Sacc!" Pupetra shouted into the darkness. Two white eyes appeared seemingly out of nowhere. "I want you to disable the domes for all games and the anti-viruses."

"Done." Sacc spoke clearly.

The viruses crashed down on the map like a meteor strike. They hit the island with enough force to send the oceans into space, leaving it obliterated worse than she ever achieved.

Within the blink of an eye, they were on the coast of the island with the sand seeping between their toes, almost like quicksand. Pupetra turned towards Kylo. Her outstretched hand went from an open palm to a clenched fist and struck Kylo. Kylo collapsed to the ground and his motionless body turned to dust.

One of the viruses landed inches from Pupetra and immediately latched onto her. An excruciating pain followed through Pupetra, of which there was no escape, seemed to last forever. Like a lion mauls a deer, and a snake entangles its prey, the virus seemed to tighten its grip on Pupetra; the more she tried to wriggle out of its trap.

The pain came to an abrupt halt but in a flash, all the other viruses came flying at Pupetra like metal to a magnet. Feeling dizzy, Pupetra collapsed, but the sand softened the fall.

"Pupetra..." a deep ominous voice spoke.

"Who are you?! Where are you?!" Pupetra got up in a panic and felt something she was only used to putting in other people, fear.

"I am Ultra-Virus, an alter ego that now lives within you. I know what you want, your ambitions match mine so I will help you." Ultra-Virus told Pupetra as it raised her arm like a conductor in an orchestra. Immediately, all of her minions flashed before her eyes.

"Let me add to your minions and make an army." Ultra-Virus took over Pupetra's body and jets of red beams blasted out of Pupetra's chest. After Pupetra took control of her body again, she was staring into thousands of mirror reflections of... herself. "I call them puppetitans, zombie-like puppets that will obey your every command. Now let's go make some friends..." Ultra virus suggested.

A portal, created by Ultra Virus, seemed to form and appear out of nothing, staring at Pupetra; without hesitation, she and her army prowled through it.

***

Pupetra and her army suddenly found themselves aboard a ship the size of her conquered island.

The pirate's skin was of deepest ebony and her slight frame was deceptive. Her baggy clothes hid it well, but she was strong and muscular. There was clearly no better swordsman on the ship than her and if she felt you had disrespect in your tone, you would pay with your life. Her crew was named the Smiling Skulls. She was beholden to no man. She was the captain.

"Ahoy matey. The name be Melvina, Captain Melvina to ye!!" Captain Melvina announced herself as the rest of her crew attended to their duties.

"What business do ye have on mi ship?" She questioned.

"How would you like to defy destiny…" Pupetra spoke with such confidence and so clearly everyone seemed to follow her exact words, disregarding Captain Melvina's speech. "There is only so much you can do in this virtual world, but what if I were to tell you that with my help, we can escape this world and conquer the real world together? Are you on board?"

Captain Melvina seemed to eye Pupetra up and down multiple times. The fact that a stranger seemed to march on her ship as if *she* was the captain angered Captain Melvina from the inside. She was boiling like an active volcano. But the look on her face seemed to say it all. She was as bewildered as everyone else on the ship at what Pupetra had just offered.

"Have you lost ye mind? This is my ship. Don't you ever try to undermine my words again. Got it?" Captain Melvina fired back.

"Are you on board or not, Melvina?" Pupetra mocked. Instantly Captain Melvina drew her sword from her belt to hold it up centimetres from Pupetra's neck.

"Captain Melvina to ye!!!" Captain Melvina smiled and nodded to herself to find Pupetra didn't move a muscle within those second. "If this is going to work, we need to recruit as many villains from different games,"

"Agreed" Pupetra acknowledged. It's not that those on board the boat expected smooth sailing, or for winds to be kind, the waves to be gentle; it's that they trusted our ship to carry them to shore no matter the weather. It was a confidence born of faith, of feeling to their bones that with such tenacity we could achieve anything at all. They say it's only impossible until it's done. That was the motto under all skies, upon all seas. They believed we could do anything at all, and so they did.

The same portal appeared out of nothing to stare at everyone on board the ship. Pupetra and her army led the way, with Captain Melvina and the Smiling Skulls following.

***

The castle walls are the strongest thing for miles around, yet when Pupetra looks carefully, she notices the stones are not actual stones; they are Lego bricks. Built of stones of varying sizes and shapes, each one unique. From a distance it is uniform grey, from up close it is a mosaic of humble rocks. The more Pupetra looked around, she seemed to notice that everything appeared to be made of Lego.

Pupetra and her now expanded army stood upon the drawbridge, which was the entrance to the grand, expansive castle. At one time, this was where the horses passed over, where they carried the goods into the citadel within. This was more than a castle; it was a home for everyone in these parts.

One man seemed to appear out of nothing before the eyes of everyone on the drawbridge. Without hesitation, Zane, a member of Captain Melvina's crew, ran fearlessly at the unknown man. He dodged all the swings of the sword from Zane and simply touched his hand. Just like that, Zane turned into a Lego statue.

"You seem like a being of dominant power… but imagine how powerful you'd be with an army of the most elite?" Pupetra proposed to the man.

"Go on,"

"So, will you join me and help conquer the real world?" Pupetra offered.

"The name is Leogo, and you are?" he asked.

"Pupetra. Oh, and that woman with the sword and the weirdly shaped black hat is Melvina," Pupetra introduced. But if looks could kill, Captain Melvina would have made Pupetra suffer an insurmountable amount of pain by torturing her.

"Don't worry Captain, in time we will make her pay," One of her crew members whispered to her.

"Don't worry about James. We will control her strings soon enough," Captain Melvina laughed to herself.

***

It wasn't long before Pupetra and her new army managed to assemble a team of villains from various games created by Tadeo. Many villains rejected the idea because they felt going out would be too risky playing with the laws of code.

Because of this, most of them had to pay a price courtesy of Pupetra. The new villains Pupetra got on board were Mothman and Miss Smasher.

Mothman was literally a mutated moth that stood on two feet and built a moth-like suit, giving him enhanced flying abilities. Mothman also could communicate with and control a spider army general called Arachnis, and since he controlled the general, he could control the whole spider army.

Miss Smasher was a woman with mud-coloured hair but had a red complexion and white eyes. She only has one goal; she has only ever had one goal, to destroy everything and everyone. Luckily, Pupetra had the abilities of how to manipulate the Miss Smasher.

"Today we will go to the real world," Pupetra directed her new empire. "And today we start our mission to erase all humans from existence."

Chapter 3

In Pupetra's mind, she had already taken over the enormous area in which Tadeo lives, called Walden. Walden was on the outskirts of London, it was just like your average town and offered many houses, shopping centres, flats, corner shops and more.

Walden was well known for having the largest air-force base in the world. Although cars and tanks were at the military base, the speed and size of the jets and planes built in Walden are unmatched.

"The chase is on Tadeo, and I will find you. I will hunt you down like prey and erase anyone remotely connected to you. Don't think you can evade me forever; you are already in my territory." Pupetra recited her plan in her head.

Her empire was in hot pursuit, hurdling over fallen trees and buildings reduced to rubble. At the center of it was Pupetra, mad with insurmountable power. A purple oozy energy fired like jets from her palms and would disintegrate anyone who challenged her to ash.

Tadeo's eyes open like two flashlight beams. His eyes took in every ray of light; though they were open, he couldn't think of why. His heart was pounding, yet his mind was empty.

He slowly rubbed his fingers along the silken mattress. He pressed his cheek to the cool velvet pillows. Warmth and darkness enveloped Tadeo in his royal-like bed.

Seemed to be a typical morning as his parents would be in a hotel in central London to attend a court trial to support one of their friends for a motorbike accident. Meanwhile, Nia stayed with Aunty Michelle.

Noises are in full swing, traffic heavy as expected. But today it matched the noises with an intense stream of screams and shouts. Car alarms going off added to the mix of all this commotion.

After finishing his breakfast, Tadeo walked back upstairs and turned on his Gamechip 64 to play the latest Fifa. As an Arsenal supporter through and through, Tadeo wanted to use as many Arsenal players as he could in his ultimate team. As the Gamechip 64 loaded up, Tadeo thought of how being home alone most Saturdays for a while benefited him, as he had to learn responsibility and independence.

Logging into his account on the Gamechip 64, Tadeo had never noticed how time is so much like water; that it can pass slowly, a drop at a time, even freeze, or rush by in a blink.

The list of games came up; it was a sight of pure horror. There were no games. None. On the whole console, there were no games.

"What! How, it's like I have deleted them…." Tadeo said, burying his hands in his head.

Seconds later, the subtle yet clear sound of broken glass caught his ear. Instantly, an anxious Tadeo dashed out of his room to the landing. From the top of the stairs, he could see that the front door had been through trauma, punched and kicked.

A mutant with a red complexion was now in Tadeo's line of sight.

"I've found the boy, Pupetra," Miss Smasher told her via a communications watch on her wrist.

Tadeo made a run for it; sprinting in his room, he locked his door behind him. He opened his window and took a leap of faith. Tadeo landed in a crouched position, on his toes, and took a few strides to keep his balance safely. As he had taken many parkour classes over the summer, Tadeo ran to the corner of his garden behind the shed and pushed his body through the fox hole which led him to the side road behind his house.

Smelling the stench of the mutant he knew was right behind him, Tadeo bolted down the road when he saw what looked like a strange group of puppet-like zombies, which looked familiar. Confused, shocked and scared, Tadeo was surrounded.

"My lord!" a voice spoke from behind. "Get in quickly!"

Tadeo recognised that voice anywhere. It was Sliftu in the back of a police van. Without hesitation, Tadeo ran into the van and sped off past the puppetitans and took a sharp left. In the front seat was Barboach and driving was Clitho.

"Guys!" Tadeo sighed in relief. "I've never been happier to see you. But what are you doing here? And how did you get out of the game?"

"I'll tell him," Clitho began "Long story short, Pupetra could hack the code so she could come into the real world. And she has help from other villains from other games that you made. So each game deleted themselves, but luckily this little guy saved us and other heroes from other games; and brought us to the real world too."

"Oh, wow. But who are you talking about?"

A small blue ooze shaped a figure emerged from under Tadeo's seat the height of toddler

"Me, I'm Anti virus. You can call me AV. When Pupetra hacked the code, I was temporarily disabled, but as the games deleted themselves, I saved as many heroes as I could."

"Hi, I guess," Tadeo silently laughed to himself in disbelief, "Where are we going, anyway?"

"We saw this place we think would be a good base for us to set up. The other heroes are there as well," Barboach said.

The police van rammed into the gates of a car park. Tadeo noticed it was his school, Westwood High.

"This is my school! Way to be subtle, Clitho." Tadeo commented with his arms crossed. Clitho, Barboach and Sliftu led Tadeo into the sports hall -ironicly- where his eyes met recognisable faces.

"Ello captain Tadeo," said a boy who stepped forward, looking not much older than Tadeo. "The name's Flint, may not look like I can do much. But I can pack a punch,"

Flint's eyes turned to a flame orange, and he transformed into a dragon in a split second. He had a menacing look about him. Flint, in dragon form, stood no bigger than a fully grown elephant; it walked forwards; head bowed submissively.

The dragon was the colour of the night, not a coincidence, but merely a function of his multi-chromatic skin. His eyes could zoom in from hundreds of meters away and his ears could isolate sounds from one another. He could talk and mimic any creature, even the human voice.

"So, we got a metamorphic dragon!" Tadeo said as Flint turned back to his human form.

Tadeo turned his attention to this older man who looked like an army general, no older than thirty.

"At ease, soldier. Just call me CC," the man commanded."I have the power of invincibility but only when the sun is out. It charges this vest right here and I'm a human shield. I also carry these small grenades in my pocket."

Two things that would only be human-sized insects stepped forward.

"I'm Iron Wasp and I can shrink or enlarge any object. I also know every fighting style known to man."

"I'm Beetle. I can communicate with wildlife and can control most insects. Some I can't talk to though,"

A woman then tapped Tadeo on the back, waiting to introduce herself

"All you need to know is that I can create something out of nothing," said this girl, who looked like she had just finished school. She had a chocolate skin tone with fine braids and wore an iced out watch with a necklace with the pendant 'N'. "I'm Nyla"

"Nice to meet you, Nyla, I'm…" as Tadeo was introducing himself, familiar faces burst into the sports hall. All of them were out of breath. A couple of people from Tadeo's year ran over to him, all looking confused but relieved.

"Yo, Tadeo, what are you doing here?" Andre ran over to his friend, along with Kiara.

"I think the better question is, who are you with?" Mason fired at him

"This is Clitho, Barboach, and Sliftu." Tadeo introduced

"So, they're all freaks like you then." Mason mocked.

"Takes one to know one though, right?" Tadeo asked.

"Why you gotta get into him like that, bro? Just leave the guy alone," Nathan told Mason.

"Whatever," Mason shrugged, then directing his attention at Barboach "But I'm staring at a weasel standing on two feet, so explain. We've all just had to run for our lives. And can someone please explain to me why there are puppet zombies after us."

"They came from a game I made. And those puppet zombies may have something to do with the game as well. From all the games I've made, the bad guys escaped."

"So how are we gonna stop these guys?" Jake asked.

"We need more people with us if we are going to take them on." Kiara suggested. "We could broadcast a message by the Channel 7 station down the road. My mum works there so I know how to do it,"

"Kiara is right, but we can't all go to the station. We will all get spotted. Half of us should go and broadcast the message to anyone still out there." Tadeo explained. He stopped and thought for a moment. "You guys don't really seem fazed about what's in this hall, you know?"

"Seeing as we have all seen our town in ruins and chased by zombies, not the weirdest thing we have seen today." Nathan spoke on behalf of his small group. The others nodded in agreement.

"Who's with me and going to Channel 7's station?" Tadeo bravely asked his associates who stood in the sports hall.

Many raised their hands, some said nothing. But he had enough people to carry out their plan.

Chapter 4

They travelled in one silver, clean Mercedes which they accessed through the teachers' only car park. Most of the teachers left their cars there over the weekend. CC drove with Kiara in the passenger's seat. Tadeo, Nathan and Nyla all remained in the three back

seats. Everyone else stayed behind as going in the police van would make them easily identifiable.

Although calm and composed behind the wheel, CC drove like a madman. Despite travelling to the news station using the sideroads, they arrived within minutes. All

Tadeo saw were rapid blurs of the concrete jungle he called home.

Channel 7 station looked like they started building a hotel but changed their minds midway through building and built many small houses. They parked up and Kiara led the way.

Large French doors, followed by a white carpet, had the feel of sand even under everyone's shoes. Tadeo, Kiara and Nathan trekked up the emerald stairs into the broadcasting room, whilst Nyla guarded the door on the other side and downstairs CC guarded the main door.

Kiara hacked the system so the televisions and radios throughout the town's system would hear this message. Nathan held the camera like a professional. He gave Tadeo the signal to begin.

"For anyone still out there listening to this, make your way to Westwood High. These are troubling times but together we can win against these beasts around our town." Tadeo felt a fresh surge of hope.

"Bravery, I rate that," Nathan told Tadeo as he put the camera down.

"Through the back door! We've been followed!!! MOVE MOVE MOVE." CC burst inside, barricading the doors behind him.

"No. I've got this. Pass me anything in here and I will build our way out of here," Nyla commanded.

Tadeo, Nathan and Kiara did so without hesitation, whilst CC obviously knew that this was a bad idea. From his point of view, it was about survival. He ran upstairs to the broadcasting room and left the other four behind without saying a word.

No one knew how, but in the space of a couple of seconds, from tearing parts of inside the news station down, Nyla had built a car with a drill, bigger than an elephant, at the front.

Everyone scrambled in the car. The broadcasting room door flung open, windows smashing as the puppetitans erupted through. The car drill seemed to spin out of control and drilled through the earth's crust - they were underground, creating a path for themselves.

"What about CC?" Tadeo questioned

"He left us, and he should've come with us," Nyla said authoritatively.

"How do you know where you are going? It's just mud and rocks around us down here. I can't see a thing," Nathan asked impatiently, as sweat ran down his forehead onto his clothes.

"I put a tracking device on the school. Trust me, I know what I'm doing." Nyla smiled at all of them.

Captain Melvina, her crew, and Mothman stood still, peering down at the enormous hole that was now at the news station created by Nyla's car. It appeared bottomless, with an inviting sense of mystery to it.

One puppetitan tripped over the side and somersaulted down as if it was a gymnastics competition. It wasn't until seconds later that they would hear a thud, sounding as if someone had been slapped across the face; viciously.

"Your highness," Mothman held down the earpiece to speak to Pupetra. "We know where they are heading."

"Forget about it." Pupetra dictated. "I am sending you coordinates now... BRING EVERYONE." She cut off the call without an answer from Mothman.

"You heard the empress, let's move..."

An elderly woman unexpectedly entered the news station and like how a pack of predators saw prey, all eyes were on her. Preserved in a position which could only be described as raw trepidation. Captain Melvina and her crew, Mothman and all the Puppetitans stared at the woman with viciousness in all their eyes.

A swarm of Puppetitans emerged forward, two of them grabbed each of her arms. Another stepped forward and placed its hand on her forehead; the woman's eyes lit up to a freakishly dark purple. Her skin peeled like an onion. She was now looking into a reflection. She was now a puppetitan.

CC was upstairs in the radio station surrounded, almost submerged by rubbish and old technology. He peered in through the window and was able to see the exact coordinates as a hologram; and able to see the horror of what had just happened with the elderly woman still going undetected.

The puppetitans, Mothman, Captain Melvina, and her crew all vacated the building abruptly in persuit of Tadeo.

CC rambled into his pocket and got his phone out and immediately tried to get on the phone to Nyla.

"Hello, Nyla. Come in Nyla…" CC spoke as clearly as he could.

"Yeah, we can all hear you loud and clear. We made it back to the school." Tadeo informed him.

"No one is going to help us win this fight. It's just us." CC broke the news with no form of stuttering.

"What?!" Everyone sounded both in shock and as if a blow had been dealt to the stomach.

"The zombies can turn more people to look like them. The entire town could be zombies for all we know. But listen up! I know where they are heading, and I am sending you their coordinates now," CC stated to the team.

"They're trying to go to the air force base!!!" Kiara gasped

"Wait. The group of them that left the channel station a second ago have to go past the bridge, right?" CC asked.

"With those planes and jets, it's not just our town... it's the *world*." Nathan explained.

"Trap them at the base." Clitho demanded.

"I'll go with CC. He can't take on half the army alone." Flint offered.

"Flint will go with CC at the bridge and the rest of us will get to the air force base. Everyone move, now!" Tadeo nodded

"I'm on it," CC ended the call.

Ascending through the air in his dragon form, Flint thought of himself as just a bigger bird. Although free, he felt isolated that there was no one like him in or out of a game. Other times, being so high in the mountains would allow him to feel unique.

Flint's scaly body now a brilliant white, soared across the skies. The silver linings of the clouds were being sliced by vast, beautiful wings. The figure stood prominent in the bright cosmic-looking sky above, with only small pockets of clouds where he wouldn't be detected.

Tracking down the raw stench of CC's constant sweat wasn't hard enough for Flint as he descended further and further down.

Captain Melvina, her crew, Mothman and all the puppetitans were close to the bridge, moving as a wave in the sea. They called it the Crystal crossing, once upon a time. A hundred years ago, the bridge was built with skill and precision right above the usually tranquil river. They say it was made by the Windrush generation. Each block was square and perfectly laid, the arches were mathematical semi-circles and along the edges were admirable.

CC was stealthily trying to keep his distance yet remain as close as could be.

Flint skydived right into a large garbage council van with enough litter to break his fall; he still thought he smelt better than CC.

"OI, CC!" Flint tried to have as loud a whisper as possible, now transformed back into a human

"Dragon?" CC came out from the little alleyway he was hiding in.

"Listen, we have to take these guys out, but you have to do exactly as I say." Flint extended his hand.

"Brave and straightforward. Let's do this," CC agreed and shook his hand.

The road lay on the bridge as an endless river of tarmac baked under a relentless sun. It stretched into the horizon in front and behind as far as the eye can see. The once black tarmac was now grey with dust.

The smaller army all moved like a wave across the bridge. A plume of fire exploded onto the road as the flames pummelled out from Flint's mouth as he flew over the bridge, with CC on his back. The inferno illuminated the bridge, and they were now surrounded by a blaze.

"Look, it's a dragon!" Mothman drew everyone's attention to Flint and CC.

"Fend for yourselves, I have got this," Captain Melvina drew her sword, seemingly ignoring the fact that Flint and CC were in the air.

Many of the puppetitans tried to run through the fire, but they were immediately disintegrated and erased.

The bridge dropped, just like that... darker blue and green seeped and oozed into the water below, making it seem swamp like from where Flint and CC were.

They travelled in two vans; this 'army' was all that stood in the way of Pupetra and her goal. The air force base seemed almost extinct, but that was in their favour.

Mason, Nathan and Andre all scavenged the air force base to find all kinds of madness. Their eyes just lit up like fireworks as the door opened. Nathan ransacked the place, finding many explosive grenades. Mason's instinct drew him towards a single baseball bat in the corner of the room. Andre broke open a glass case on the wall to find a weirdly designed gun. Accidentally, he pressed the trigger and a beam of blue light hurled at the wall, leaving a huge whole. With all of them now smiling, they left the camp to regroup with the others. Meanwhile, Tadeo crafted a bullet in one of the more sciences looking labs further down the air force base, whilst his friends tried to gather their gear.

Nyla, with the old bits and bobs that she had found, had built herself a robot the size of two basketball players. She was able to control with a ring on her wrist that synced with the robot.

However, Tadeo and Kiara could hack one of the fighter jets with a machine gun attached. They also managed to make sure the jet couldn't fly as the Puppetitans would not be able to pilot it. After a few alterations, they successfully managed to disable the jet. The team was now a solid, united, firm wall.

Tadeo and Kiara drove the jet onto the runway, nearest to the gate where they all stood. Nathan, Mason, and Andre looked locked and loaded. Nyla had her robot in front of her in a stance, as if it was going for boxing. Beetle, Iron Wasp, Sliftu, Barboach, Clitho had fire in their eyes, peeking over the horizon to see when Pupetra would emerge.

The acrid stench of rot met Tadeo's nose.

"It smells like hell to me," he told the rest of them through his earpiece he had found around the base.

Under the chill of the mist, everyone could sense Pupetra and her army.

The puppetitan army moved as one, a sea of green, as if there were just one brain instead of many. The right legs moved in unison and then the left legs. With each step, the sound they made on the cold tarmac was like the warning thunder of a coming storm.

They were now distinctly in sight. Even through the grand front window of the jet, it was as if Pupetra was staring right into the soul of Tadeo.

"ERASE THEM!!!" The shriek flew from Pupetra's mouth.

Miss Smasher wasted no time. Like an untamed bull, she charged at the jet where Tadeo and Kiara let loose, holding the trigger of the machine gun, which didn't seem to do much. Out of nowhere, a forcefield burst around the jet, rocketing her in the opposite direction.

"Remember about me?" a small figure emerged from the corner of the jet.

"AV! Thank God." Tadeo was relieved

"Listen exactly as I say…" AV commanded

An all-out war erupted. No one was backing down from either side. All the puppetitans were brain dead but proved as target practice for Nathan, Mason and Andre, who were all fuelled by bravery.

Nyla had her robot doing all of her dirty work; brushing aside Arachnis and the spider army.

Leogo the Lego king, was surrounded by Clitho, Sliftu and Barboach. Despite being cornered, he extended his hand and immediately Barboach turned to a Lego statue, with a facial expression being lifeless. Pure horror was now on the face of the other two fighting.

Consumed with vengeance, Clitho kept on dodging the attacks left, right and centre until he couldn't. He flung himself forward in anger and he too suffered the same fate and was caught by Leogo. Sliftu closed his eyes whilst tapping his staff on the ground as if he was commanding something to continue fighting so his two dearest friends would not be in vain.

Just like that, Barboach was sucked into the earth like prey to a predator. Gone. Sliftu had no time to mourn with the puppetitans creeping up behind him somewhat playfully with a hint of menace about them.

Pupetra herself remained a conductor, with purple ooze being launched from her hands. A howl of pain screamed from Nyla as her robot was hit, collapsed and was now a pile of rubble, a blanket on top of her. All because of the brute power the Pupetra now wielded with Ultra virus feeding her this new strength.

Although Pupetra now had power, which now made her 'happy', satisfaction was not even a possibility for Pupetra, never. Her army was falling. Looking around, she knew what she had to do. She raised her hand. Even in war, she seemed abnormal, pointing to the heavens.

The puppetitans stopped the fighting abruptly and moved faster than they ever had before, surrounding and submerging her as if she was being attacked. It was the complete opposite. Like a pack of lions, they ran around in a perfect circular motion continuously.

Tadeo and Kiara ran outside the jet with a sniper in hand and regrouped with what was left of their comrades. Nathan barely had a scratch on him. Mason and Andre were the same. Sliftu pointed to the statues of his fallen comrades. Nyla was nowhere to be seen. They all stood a few metres from a pile of ash, which everyone assumed to be iron wasp and beetle who were erased in battle.

"This is it?" Nathan's voice trembled. A confused Tadeo looked at him as if he had just seen a ghost.

"Wait, look!!!" Kiara exclaimed.

Pupetra was now a giant standing at one hundred feet, towering over Tadeo and his friends below.

Flint, in his dragon form, was hurtling towards Pupetra with CC on his back. CC jumped off and sky dived towards his allies whilst Pupetra snatched Flint; opened her mouth and Flint was digested like a fly to a hungry frog.

"We can't beat her!" Mason cried out

"Get a grip! Get back into that jet." Tadeo snapped Mason out of it.

Everyone dashed into the jet without a second invitation, but Tadeo stayed out and locked them all in with the keys he had kept in his pocket

"Bro, what are you doing?" Kiara screamed.

"Get out of here," Tadeo commanded.

"Tadeo!!! WHAT ARE YOU DOING?" Sliftu stressed.

"I was jealous of you, Tadeo. I... I am very sorry." Nathan gave him a sincere apology, where his voice faded.

Tadeo knew what he had to do. Pupetra was lifting the roof of the camps like they were toy houses. Although her eyes were massive now, she had finished having her fun and glared at Tadeo, sneering at him.

Tadeo got down on his knees and found the sniper, his hands quaking. He aimed and fired the bullet into her chest.

"Really!!!" Pupetra laughed. "You think a single bullet can..."

She noticed something unusual. Pupetra's complexion was going from a purple/red to a light blue. Her chest glowed a vibrant blue and Pupetra was now buzzing like a bee.

Tadeo was enjoying this from below as Pupetra shrunk and went from being a giant, touching the clouds to looking at him directly at eye level.

"That wasn't so much of a bullet, more so an anti-virus." Tadeo studied Pupetra.

The blue figure zipped around all the puppetitans, turning them back to normal humans. reducing Pupetra to nothing but a small puppet. All the puppetitans and the game characters pixelated and disappeared.

Tadeo's shoulders dropped. He didn't get to say goodbye. Tadeo grabbed the small puppet... but now he was in his room? A strange case of déjà vu fell upon him.

"I thought it would be best to undo everything she did. All of your friends still have memories of the events, though," AV told Tadeo.

"Wise choice. Thank you!" Tadeo smiled at AV. "I'm going to destroy it. The Gamechip 64. It's a madness."Just then Tadeo's phone rang, it's Nathan.

"Did that really just happen?" Nathan asked, sounding amazed and at the same time extremely concerned.

"I'm almost one hundred percent sure I wasn't dreaming!" Tadeo joked around.

"That felt like a game," Nathan ironically pointed out

"Yeah. But anyway, do you want to come over and play -" Tadeo stopped himself, he was about to ask Nathan if he wanted to play on the Gamechip 64 but he was hit with a profound realisation. "Football?"

"Yeah, I'll be over in twenty!" Nathan hung up.

Tadeo jumped out of his bed and, with a sense of anger yet sympathy, unplugged the wires. For all the memories that he has had with his Gamechip 64, it was hard but the right thing to do. Dragging himself downstairs reluctantly, he gently placed the console in a black bag he found by the door. He slipped on his sliders and tossed the bag in the green bin outside, feeling like he had just thrown away a potential threat. He went back inside and closed the front door and let out an enormous sigh of relief. Launching himself onto the sofa, he turned on the TV to watch the Under 23 FA cup final – with a bold black and yellow headline reading 'Newcastle - 3 Arsenal – 0' with Tadeo silently laughing to himself.

THE END

Be sure to stay in touch with
Elijah Frederick:

www.elijahfrederick.com

@authorelijahfrederick

Go back to where it all began in...

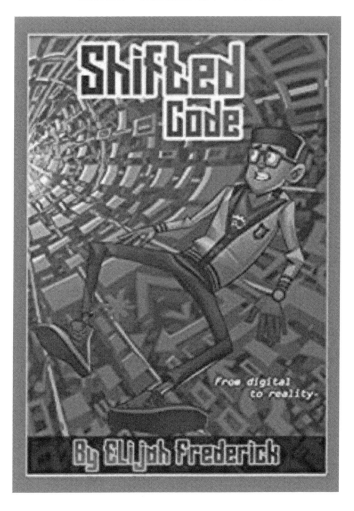

Shifted Code

Bullied by Nathan and his friends, Tadeo
was a tormented genius who was isolated
and excluded by everyone in his class.
Through an unlucky pairing in class, a
brawny Nathan and a victimised Tadeo
would have to deal with the misery of
working together on a computing project.
With Nathan constantly giving Tadeo a
hard time and making very little effort,
Tadeo is left to work on his own, only to
be sucked into the game they were
creating for the project. Tadeo finds
himself in a strange world where he learns
a terrible truth about a blood curdling
menace who has been reigning through
fear and terror.

Printed in Great Britain
by Amazon